TEDDY BEAR FARMER

by Phoebe and Joan Worthington

VIKING KESTREL

For Yves and Suzanne
With grateful thanks to Harry of Moss Farm

VIKING KESTREL
Penguin Books Ltd, Harmondsworth, Middlesex, England
Viking Penguin Inc., 40 West 23rd Street, New York, New York 10010, U.S.A.
Penguin Books Australia Ltd, Ringwood, Victoria, Australia
Penguin Books Canada Ltd, 2801 John Street, Markham, Ontario, Canada L3R 1B4
Penguin Books (N.Z.) Ltd, 182-190 Wairau Road, Auckland 10, New Zealand

First published 1985

British Library Cataloguing in Publication Data available

ISBN 0-670-80342-1

Printed in Great Britain by
William Clowes and Sons Ltd, Beccles

Once upon a time there was
a Teddy Bear Farmer.

He had a tractor,

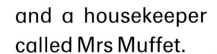

a dog

and a housekeeper
called Mrs Muffet.

The Teddy Bear Farmer got up very early in the morning and went to milk his cows. He gave them their food in their manger. Then the Teddy Bear Farmer sat on a stool to milk them. *Swish*, went the milk into the bucket. *Swish-swish, swish-swish.*

He took his churns of milk in a trailer to the gate in the road, and left them for the milk lorry to collect.

Then the Teddy Bear Farmer went back to the house
to eat the good breakfast that Mrs Muffet had cooked
for him.

After breakfast he let the hens out of the hen house, and gave them some corn.

Then he went to feed his sow and her little piglets. The
Teddy Bear Farmer and Mrs Muffet thought they were
very nice.

Next he went to the field to feed his calves.

The Teddy Bear Farmer went to the market. He bought
a nice brown and white cow and her calf.

After lunch he tossed the hay over in the little meadow so that it would dry quickly. Mrs Muffet helped him and the work was soon done.

The Teddy Bear Farmer collected the eggs and took them to the dairy. Mrs Muffet was making butter into pats to sell.

There was a knock at the dairy door. A boy had come
to buy six brown eggs and a pat of butter. He paid
the Teddy Bear Farmer ten pennies – one, two,
three, four, five, six, seven, eight, nine, ten.

It was getting dark. The Teddy Bear Farmer went round the farm to shut all the animals up for the night. He shut the hens up very carefully in case a fox came looking for supper.

The Teddy Bear Farmer was very tired. After his bath, he took his cocoa up to bed and looked at pictures in a book. Soon he was fast asleep.

And that is the story of the Teddy Bear Farmer.